Mighty, Mighty Construction Site

chronicle books · san francisco

SHERRI DUSKEY RINKER AND TOM LICHTENHELD

Down in the big construction site,
five trucks wake to morning light.
It's time to S-T-R-E-T-C-H, roll out of bed,
and gear up for the day ahead!

They wipe their faces,

greet the sun,

load up,
fuel up,

rev up... run!

They're eager to get things underway.
There's a brand-new job to start today!

The plan's unrolled. They stare in awe—
the biggest thing they ever saw.
A massive building, so immense—
this giant job will be intense!

It's a *lot* for them to do . . .
too much for just a five-truck crew?

Mighty trucks all hear the call—
they start up in no time at all!
Out on the road, they drive full steam.
They rush right in to join the team.

Rolling, rumbling, revving hard,
ten big trucks meet in the yard.
A mighty, massive SUPERCREW—
there is *nothing* they can't do!

Skid Steer's nimble,

small, and quick.

She turns,
she spins—

she does a trick!

Bulldozer's heavy, wide, and grand.
He'll push and plow to clear the land . . .
but even *he* can use a hand!

Skid's breaker bit blasts rocks to rubble,
so 'Dozer rolls through without trouble.
Two friends at work—one big, one small;
they clear the way. They move it all!

Each long trench is marked and planned:
Excavator digs the land,

then Backhoe grabs a drainage pipe
and sets it down in one smooth swipe.

Turn and dig then lift and drop,
then push some dirt right back on top—
they set each pipe, and then repeat.
This duo doesn't miss a beat!

Pulling up with all his might,
Crane Truck lifts a beam to height.
And then he spins his hook around,
but just before it touches ground,
Crane Truck *gasps!* out in surprise:

He's used up all of his supplies!

But what's this coming down the road?
Could it be another load?

Mighty Flatbed revs and runs,
smoothly hauling FIFTY TONS
down the road and over hills.
Her load's strapped tight, so nothing spills.

On site,
she rolls right to a stop,
with Crane's supplies
all stacked on top.

Flatbed Truck's
just saved the day!
Their work can get
back underway.

Front-End Loader and Dump Truck pair
to move great loads from here to there,
digging, lifting, hauling ground—
giant piles are moved around!

Loader digs and scoops his fill,
then tilts it up so there's no spill.
His bucket raises to the max.

Then
Beep-Beep-Beep!
as Loader backs.

Dirt and gravel hauled away,
these pals move MOUNTAINS every day!

Cement Mixer is working hard
around the whole construction yard.

Load after load,
he churns and pours,

makes foundations,
roads, and floors.

WET CEMENT!

...and here is Pumper, right on time!

Pumper's boom unfolds, goes high—
reaching *up, up* toward the sky.

Fill the hopper, flip the switch—and *zoom!*
Concrete is pushed into the boom,

up through the pipe. It does not stop.

Then concrete comes out, way up top.

Churn and pour
and lift and fill—

this team works hard
with speed and skill!

Rough and rugged all day long,
rolling, lifting, digging strong,
each truck has had a part to play
to help the work get done today.

Just like the plan—the job's complete!
This awesome team just can't be beat.
Cooperation got it done;
teamwork made it fast—and fun!

The new crew leaves—
but on their way,
Crane Truck waves.
"Great work today!"
The crew drives off,
engines loud,
feeling tired,
but strong and proud.

It's getting dark; the sun has set.
The trucks are tired as they can get!

They roll to find their cozy beds,
to cuddle up and rest their heads,
to close their eyes and drift away.
New adventures wait . . .
another day.

Construction site, all tucked in tight.

Great work today!
Now, *shh* . . . goodnight!

For my sister, Susan Goodwin: Suz, you are, always and ever, my hero.
And for The One who leads us through —S. D. R.

To teachers and librarians everywhere —T. L.

Text copyright © 2017 by Sherri Duskey Rinker.
Illustrations copyright © 2017 by Tom Lichtenheld.

Library of Congress Cataloging-in-Publication Data:
Names: Rinker, Sherri Duskey, author. | Lichtenheld, Tom, illustrator.
Title: Mighty, mighty construction site / Sherri Duskey Rinker and
Tom Lichtenheld.
Description: San Francisco, California : Chronicle Books LLC, [2017] |
Summary: Told in rhyming text, Excavator, Bulldozer, Crane Truck, Dump
Truck, and Cement Mixer will all need to work together as they tackle
their biggest job yet—a massive building.
Identifiers: LCCN 2016012070 | ISBN 9781452152165 (alk. paper)
Subjects: LCSH: Construction equipment—Juvenile fiction. | Trucks—Juvenile
fiction. | Cooperativeness—Juvenile fiction. | Stories in rhyme. | CYAC:
Stories in rhyme. | Construction equipment—Fiction. | Trucks—Fiction. |
Cooperativeness—Fiction.
Classification: LCC PZ8.3.R48123 Mi 2017 | DDC [E]—
dc23 LC record available at https://lccn.loc.gov/2016012070

Manufactured in China.

Design by Tom Lichtenheld and Kristine Brogno.
Typeset in Mr. Eaves.
The illustrations in this book were rendered in Neocolor
wax oil pastels on Mi-Teintes paper. Digital fine-tuning
by Kristen Cella.

10 9 8 7 6 5

Chronicle Books LLC
680 Second Street
San Francisco, California 94107

Chronicle Books—we see things differently.
Become part of our community at www.chroniclekids.com.